Read all the ALADDIN QUIX books!

By Stephanie Calmenson

Our Principal Is a Frog!
Our Principal Is a Wolf!
Our Principal's in His Underwear!
Our Principal Breaks a Spell!

Royal Sweets
By Helen Perelman

Book 1: *A Royal Rescue*
Book 2: *Sugar Secrets*
Book 3: *Stolen Jewels*

A Miss Mallard Mystery
By Robert Quackenbush

Dig to Disaster
Texas Trail to Calamity
Express Train to Trouble
Stairway to Doom
Bicycle to Treachery
Gondola to Danger
Surfboard to Peril
Taxi to Intrigue

Little Goddess Girls
By Joan Holub and Suzanne Williams

Book 1: *Athena & the Magic Land*
Book 2: *Persephone & the Giant Flowers*

Welcome to ALADDIN QUIX!

If you are looking for fast, fun-to-read stories with colorful characters, lots of kid-friendly humor, easy-to-follow action, entertaining story lines, and lively illustrations, then **ALADDIN QUIX** is for you!

But wait, there's more!

If you're also looking for stories with tables of contents; word lists; about-the-book questions; 64, 80, or 96 pages; short chapters; short paragraphs; and large fonts, then **ALADDIN QUIX** is *definitely* for you!

ALADDIN QUIX: The next step between ready to reads and longer, more challenging chapter books, for readers five to eight years old.

PET PALS

Mitzy's
Homecoming

ALLISON GUTKNECHT
illustrated by ANJA GROTE

ALADDIN QUIX

New York   London   Toronto   Sydney   New Delhi

For Gypsy,

my home and my heart

ALADDIN QUIX
Simon & Schuster Children's Publishing Division
1230 Avenue of the Americas, New York, New York 10020
First Aladdin QUIX hardcover edition May 2021
Text copyright © 2021 by Allison Gutknecht
Illustrations copyright © 2021 by Anja Grote
Also available in an Aladdin QUIX paperback edition.
For information about special discounts for bulk purchases, please contact
Simon & Schuster Special Sales at 1-866-506-1949 or business@simonandschuster.com.
The Simon & Schuster Speakers Bureau can bring authors to your live event. For
more information or to book an event contact the Simon & Schuster Speakers Bureau
at 1-866-248-3049 or visit our website at www.simonspeakers.com.
Book designed by Laura Lyn DiSiena
The illustrations for this book were rendered digitally.
The text of this book was set in Archer Medium.
Manufactured in the United States of America 0421 FFG
2 4 6 8 10 9 7 5 3 1
Library of Congress Control Number 2020937985
ISBN 978-1-5344-7399-7 (hc)
ISBN 978-1-5344-7398-0 (pbk)
ISBN 978-1-5344-7400-0 (eBook)

Cast of Characters

Luna (LOO-nuh): Cranky cat at Whiskers Down the Lane Animal Shelter

Mitzy (MIT-zee): Excitable toy poodle at the shelter

Gus (GUS): Large guard dog at the shelter

Ted (TED): Manager of Whiskers Down the Lane Animal Shelter

Dustin (DUSS-ten): Boy who wants a dog

Buttons (BUT-tens): Shy kitten at the shelter

Contents

1

Four Furry Friends

"For the last time, stop licking my ears!" **Luna** hisses the warning with a twitch of her whiskers.

"They are **filthy**," **Mitzy** protests. "I am cleaning them for you." She pushes her curly white

snout through the grate separat-
ing their cages, and sticks her
tongue toward Luna.

"BLECH." Luna marches
to the far corner, out of reach of
Mitzy's slobber.

"Alert! Alert!" **Gus** springs up, his long shaggy tail straight with attention. "**Intruder** approaching! I repeat, intruder approaching!"

"It is a kid!" Mitzy dances with excitement. "I love kids! Kids love me!"

A woman and young boy come into the lobby. Mitzy's round brown eyes beg them to meet her glance.

"Welcome to Whiskers Down the Lane Animal Shelter," **Ted** greets them. "Are you here to find a new family member?"

"My son, **Dustin**, has been begging for a dog," the woman says, placing her hand on the boy's shoulder.

"I am a dog!" Mitzy bounces higher.

"But I'm not sure he's ready for the **responsibility**," Dustin's mom continues. "So we just came to look today."

"I see," Ted begins. "Well, if you're not prepared to adopt yet, we offer a fostering program where you can bring a pet home with

you for a few days. It's like a mini-vacation for the animals so they have some time out of the shelter."

Dustin's mom nods. "I think that might be a good way for Dustin to see how much work it is to own a dog." She glances at Gus, who is still barking. "But we can't host any big dogs. Our apartment isn't large enough."

"I am small!" Mitzy squeals, her short tail wagging at top speed. "Here! Over here!"

"You're coming on a little strong,"

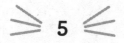

Luna observes, but Mitzy ignores her. Instead, she grips her favorite purple ball in her teeth and gives it a playful **SQUEAK**.

Dustin laughs. "Can I meet this dog?" he asks Ted.

"Yes!" Mitzy twirls in a circle. "Yes, you can!"

"Dustin, how about cats?" his mom asks. She strokes Luna's head with her finger. "They're easier to care for—yow!" She yanks her hand away. "She swiped at me!"

"Sorry. Luna can be **feisty**," Ted admits. "We also have a kitten on this side." He taps the cage beside Gus, which contains a lumpy blanket. "**Buttons** is a tad shy."

"No cat," Dustin insists. "I like dogs."

SQUEAK, SQUEAK.

Mitzy tosses her ball aside as Ted unlatches her door. Then she takes a flying leap into Dustin's arms.

"Whoa!" He wobbles as he catches her.

7

"Hello!" Mitzy pants hot breath on Dustin's face. "Do you have any treats?"

"Mitzy is a toy poodle," Ted explains. "She's very **affectionate**, and she still likes to have fun, even though she's one of our older pets. She takes a few medicines to help keep her healthy."

As he speaks, Mitzy tickles Dustin's chin with kisses, which makes him giggle. "Can we take her?" Dustin asks.

His mom shakes her head.

"Let's see who else is here first."

With an unhappy sigh, Dustin returns Mitzy to her cage and follows Ted to the back room.

A few **silent** seconds pass

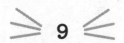

before Buttons whispers, "Are they gone?"

"Indeed," Gus answers. "I have protected us once again!"

Buttons slinks out from his blanket and spots Mitzy looking at the ground, her eyelids droopy with sadness. "What's wrong, Mitzy?"

Mitzy plops her chin onto her paws and whimpers, "I thought that boy was going to play with me. I want to run and jump and fetch my purple ball."

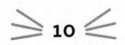

"Somebody will play with you soon," Buttons tells her. "I promise."

Mitzy turns away. "You cannot promise something that is not true."

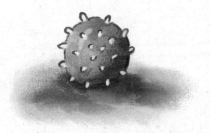

2

Bologna Boy

"Oh, quit whining!" Luna yells at Mitzy. "You wouldn't like that kid anyway. He smelled."

"Yes, like peanut butter and grass and cheese crackers," Mitzy argues. "He was delicious."

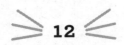

"I sniffed bologna and pow-dered doughnuts," Gus pipes up.

"He stunk of stickiness and stains," Luna insists.

"Why did Mr. Ted bring them to see the other dogs?" Mitzy asks. "We live in the lobby because we are the four best pets here. Right?"

Buttons's amber eyes widen. "Is that true, Luna?"

"Absolutely not," Luna snaps.

"Really?" Gus asks. "Why? What's wrong with us?"

Luna sprawls on her side like

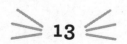

they are boring her. "Gus, you never stop barking. Humans hate barking."

"I'm a guard dog!" Gus defends himself.

"Buttons," Luna continues, focusing on the kitten, "the whole rest of your litter got adopted, but you hide whenever someone comes close. And you, Mitzy." She turns toward the cage next door.

"I am so fun!" Mitzy exclaims.

"Some would call you fun," Luna says. "Some would call you a pest.

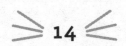

You're always begging for treats."

"Because treats are the yummi-est!" Mitzy insists.

Gus paces around his cramped space. "What about you, Luna? What's the matter with you?"

"I bite," Luna answers. "Duh."

Suddenly the door to the back room flies open. Buttons scurries under his blanket.

"Please, Mom?" Dustin begs, returning to Mitzy's cage. "She's my favorite."

"Yes!" Mitzy exclaims. "I knew he would be back!" Her nails click-clack on her cage's metal bottom as she spins with joy.

Dustin's mom **exhales** loudly. "You mentioned fostering a pet for a few days?" she asks Ted. "Would Mitzy be available for that?"

"Sure, I can arrange for you to take Mitzy home for a long weekend," Ted answers.

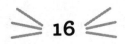

Dustin's mom turns to the boy. "What do you think? Do you want Mitzy to visit us?"

"Yes!" Dustin exclaims. "But I'm calling her Snowball."

"Snowball?" Luna sneers as

Ted unlocks Mitzy's cage.

"Is he allowed to change her name?" Gus yaps.

Mitzy bounces into Dustin's arms and licks his cheek. "He tastes amazing. Like peanut butter and grass and cheese crackers."

"I need you to fill out some paperwork." Ted steers them toward his office. "And I'll give you her daily pills."

Luna arches her back. "I don't like this. I don't like this one bit."

"Why? She'll get to run and

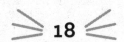

jump and fetch her purple ball," Gus points out. "Isn't that what Mitzy wants?"

"She doesn't understand what can happen," Luna answers. "What if that boy feeds her chocolate? What if he leaves the door open? What if he drops her leash?" She starts grooming her fur to calm herself. "He doesn't know how to take care of a dog. His mom said so."

"I never thought of all that," Buttons says. He tucks his tail between his legs with concern.

Gus lifts his snout and howls at the ceiling, "You better keep Mitzy safe, Bologna Boy!"

3

Missing Mouse

"I can't believe they didn't take her purple ball." Buttons speaks to the shadows of Whiskers Down the Lane. It's the middle of the night, but Mitzy's friends can't sleep.

"Maybe Bologna Boy will buy

her new toys," Gus suggests.

"But she was so looking forward to fetching her ball," Buttons says. "I don't think she's ever been away from it before. Has she, Luna?"

Rather than answering, Luna strolls to her litter box and scrapes the surface before changing her mind. She turns toward her stuffed mouse and whacks it hard enough to send it sailing through the bars and onto the floor.

"Oh no!" Buttons gasps. "Your mouse!"

"**EEEEEK!**" Gus squeaks. "Where's the mouse? Where?" Each strand of his wild fur seems to stand on end.

Luna studies him curiously.

"You, the great guard dog, are afraid . . . of mice?" she asks.

Gus stills himself. "I am not afraid of anything! I was just wondering about the mouse's location. So I could catch it."

"Yeah, sure you were," Luna scoffs. She folds her front paws beneath her body so that she **resembles** a loaf of bread. Then she squints her eyes closed.

"Psssst, Buttons," Gus whispers, hoping Luna can't hear him. "Where exactly is the mouse? You

know dogs don't see as well in the dark as cats."

Buttons reaches out his tiny paw and places it on Gus's knee. "Don't be scared. Luna knocked her toy mouse onto the floor."

Gus releases a deep breath. "I was not scared!" he lies. "But why did she hit her toy?"

"I think she's still nervous about Mitzy being away," Buttons says. "Maybe if we figure out how to get Mitzy her ball, we could check on her at the same time. Knowing

that Mitzy is okay should make Luna feel better."

Gus straightens, his ears perked into points. "So we need to find where Bologna Boy lives? That won't be a problem. I can follow the scent of bologna and powdered doughnuts." He throws himself against the door of his cage, but it doesn't budge.

"You're going to hurt yourself!" Buttons scolds. "Give me a minute." He lies on his back and extends one leg toward his lock. Once

his claws touch it, he jingles the handle up, then he jangles it over, then he pushes his door wide open. "Yippee!" He dives to the ground.

"You are a magician!" Gus exclaims.

"It's no big deal. I watch Ted do it every day." Buttons starts jingling and jangling the latch on Gus's cage, until it unlocks.

"**Genius**!" Gus bounds out and slides across the slick tiles. "I am off to locate Mitzy!" He puts his snout to the floor and snorts

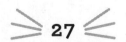

loudly. Then he follows a zigzag trail into Ted's office.

Buttons tiptoes over to the toy mouse. He lifts it by the tail and carries it to Luna, placing it beside her.

"Now you're not alone," Buttons whispers.

4

An Expected Visitor

Luna opens her eyes slowly, glaring at the first hints of morning light shining into the lobby. She peers across the room and finds two empty cages where Gus and Buttons should be. Alarmed, her

tail poofs out like a stick of cotton candy. She crouches down and lets out a low growl.

"Yeeeeeeeep!"
SWOOSH.
THUD.
CRASH!
"Hissssssssssss."

"Guard dog on duty! Guard dog on duty!" Gus is startled awake. He stands tall by his post next to the front door, howling at the knob and waiting for the intruder.

"Wait." He stops barking. "No

one is here." He turns and finds
loose papers scattering the floor.
An empty vase sits beside three
fallen plastic flowers. Buttons bal-
ances unsteadily on the computer
keyboard.

"It was an accident," Buttons says meekly. He bounds to the ground and paws at the papers, trying to gather them like a mountain of litter.

"What's going on?" Luna shrieks.

"I thought you were still asleep," Buttons explains. "So when you growled, I got surprised and knocked—"

"I mean, why are you out of your cages?" Luna cuts him off.

Buttons glances at Gus, unsure if they should tell the truth.

"Spill it!" Luna slaps the side of her water bowl.

"Okay, okay." Buttons gives in. "We're figuring out where Mitzy went."

"Huh?" Luna says, confused. "That stinky boy took her home."

"But we don't know where he lives," Buttons says. "Gus tried to track his scent, but that didn't work very well. Plus, the front door is locked, and we can't find the keys. So now we have a new plan. Show her, Gus."

Gus steps away from the door, revealing that Mitzy's purple ball is resting in the middle of the welcome mat. "I'm making sure it doesn't roll out of place before Ted arrives," he tells them. "This way, as soon as he comes in, his foot will land on top of it. Its squeak will remind him that they forgot to pack Mitzy's ball. And he will make Bologna Boy bring her back."

Luna turns from one to the other, her whiskers spread wide.

After a beat, she blares, "WHY?"

Buttons lowers his head. "We want to make sure Mitzy is okay. So you won't be as worried about her."

"You don't seem like yourself with Mitzy away," Gus pipes up. "So we thought—"

"I'm fine," Luna interrupts him. "Now if you'll excuse me, I need to use the bathroom. And I suggest you clean up this mess and get back to where you belong." With a flick of her tail, she stomps into her litter box.

Gus and Buttons remain still for a moment. Then Buttons grasps a flower stem between his teeth. He flies back up to the counter and drops it on the surface.

"Can you help me with the vase?" he asks Gus.

The dog lifts the container in his mouth and places it beside Buttons. Then he bends and nibbles at the papers, crumpling one sheet into a wrinkled, gooey ball.

"Should I eat it?" he asks.

"No! You'll make yourself sick," Buttons answers. "We need to hide them."

"I'm on it!" Gus declares. He chews three more sheets into rumpled, slimy balls before carrying them into Ted's office.

Buttons grabs the flower by the petals and moves it to the right. Then he shimmies it to the left. But he can't find the correct angle to drop it into the vase.

"You'd better hurry," Luna pipes up. "Ted will be here any minute."

Gus sprints back to the lobby and fetches more papers. Buttons hauls the other flowers up to the counter, and then he thumps the vase onto its side. One by one, he bats the stems into the hole.

"Gus, can you stand this up?" he calls frantically.

The dog glides into the room. "I'm on it!" he announces. Gus widens his jaw around the vase just as two headlight beams shine through the window.

When Ted enters, he steps over Mitzy's ball without spotting it.

"Good morning, you three," he greets them. "I'll be back soon with your breakfasts." He heads into the storage closet.

"What do we do now?" Gus cries. "He didn't notice the ball."

"Let's hope he doesn't notice the crushed-up papers under his desk either," Buttons says.

Gus rams his nose through the grate. "If you unlock my cage again, I can—"

He pauses at the sound of crunching gravel. "Alert! Alert! Intruder approaching! I repeat, intruder approaching!" Buttons dives under his blanket.

"QUIET!" Luna sneers. But Gus continues barking as a fuzzy white cloud comes into the lobby. It skids across the floor in a click-clack of activity.

"Guys, great news!" the fluffy form calls.

"Mitzy?" Gus yelps.

Buttons pokes one eye out

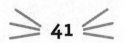

cautiously. "Mitzy!" he exclaims.

"It is me!" Mitzy scampers over to Luna and slips her tongue through the grid. "Come here. Your ears are filthy."

"BLECH." Luna stays out of Mitzy's reach, but she swishes her tail like she's waving hello.

Mitzy hops like an excitable bunny. "What happened while I was gone? Did you get any treats? Did you save some for me? Ooh, my ball!" She dashes toward her toy.

But before she can grab it, Dustin scoops her into his arms.

"Come back here, Snowball," he says. "This will only take a minute, and then we can go home again."

5

Comings and Goings

"You forgot Mitzy's purple ball yesterday!" Gus barks at Dustin. "That was not very responsible!"

Ted runs into the lobby. "What's all this noise—? Oh." His face falls

when he sees Mitzy. "One night was enough?"

"Sorry, some of Mitzy's pills wound up falling down the sink drain," Dustin's mom explains. She shoots a fast glance at Dustin, whose cheeks blush pink. "Could we get replacements?"

"Of course!" Ted says. "How is the visit going?"

"Great!" Dustin answers as Mitzy wiggles in his clutch.

"None of us slept much last

night," his mom reveals, "but I suppose that's normal?"

"Yes, a few jitters make sense," Ted says. "Let me grab extra medicine for you." He heads into his office, and Mitzy continues to squirm in Dustin's arms.

"How about if you let her walk?" his mom suggests. "She has a lot of energy."

Dustin lowers Mitzy to the floor, and she immediately sprints to Luna's cage.

"Snowball!" Dustin jogs after

her and grasps her around the ribs, and then he cradles her on his side like a football. "Here, we can look at the cat together." He leans forward so they're eye level with Luna, and Dustin sticks his nose between the metal spokes.

Luna stares at him for a moment. Then with one fierce whip, she swats at his nostrils.

"Yow!" Dustin squeals, stumbling backward.

His mom whirls around. "What happened?"

"That cat tried to scratch me!" Dustin tattles.

Mitzy licks Dustin's nose. "Luna did not mean it!" she defends her friend.

"Oh yes, I did," Luna hisses.

"Let me see." Dustin's mom

studies him. "She didn't leave a mark."

Ted enters, rattling a pill bottle. "Here you go!" He hands it to Dustin's mom.

"Thank you," she says. "Just so you know, that gray cat swiped at Dustin."

"Served him right," Luna mutters.

"Oh dear," Ted says. "We're working on Luna's social skills. Are you okay, Dustin?"

Dustin nods. "I'm fine. Snowball

already washed my nose for me." He shakes Mitzy's paw as they exit. "Say goodbye, Snowball!"

"Hey! You left the ball again!" Gus yaps, flinging himself against his door. "Buttons, unlock this thing. I have the scent this time. I can catch them!"

"That's enough, Gus," Ted says before returning to breakfast duties.

Buttons crawls all the way out from his blanket. "Mitzy seemed happy. Maybe she won't miss her

ball for a couple more days?"

"Maybe she won't miss us either," Luna mumbles.

"What did you say?" Gus asks. "I couldn't hear you."

Luna doesn't respond. Instead, she coils herself like a sleeping snake and tucks her mouse under her chin.

"Psssst," Buttons whispers to Gus. "Luna is holding on to the mouse."

"Mouse?" Gus's legs tremble and his black eyes dart around the room. "Where's the mouse? I thought the mouse was gone."

Luna growls, whacking the toy into Mitzy's cage. "It's *fake*!"

"Gus, remember?" Buttons says kindly. "It's not a real mouse."

"Of course I know that!" Gus lies. "But then why . . ." He trails off.

"Why what?" Buttons prods him.

"Why does Luna keep it?" Gus

asks. "She's had it as long as we've known her."

"That's none of your business," Luna snaps.

"But it's true," Buttons says quietly. "It must be special to you."

Luna sniffs. "It's only a silly toy."

With that, she turns her back on them, preventing any more questions.

6

Homeward Bound

Luna remains silent for hours, without a single meow or hiss.

"I'm worried," Buttons tells Gus as the sun sets outside the shelter windows. "Do you think Luna is all right?" But before

Gus can reply, the front door flies open, and a fuzzy white cloud spins into Whiskers Down the Lane.

"Intruder! Intruder!" Gus barks.

The cloud slips across the floor. "Guys, great news!"

"It's Mitzy!" Buttons exclaims, not bothering to hide. "Luna, Mitzy's here!"

"Oh dear," Ted greets Dustin and his mom. "Are things not going well?"

"This might sound strange," Dustin's mom begins, "but could you unlock her cage? We'd like to do an **experiment**."

"Okay . . . ," Ted agrees. He crosses the room and props the door open. Without delay, Mitzy leaps in and grabs her purple ball. **SQUEAK, SQUEAK.** She drops it near Luna.

"Play with me," she pants.

Luna looks from Mitzy to the ball and back again. Then, with a fast swipe, she whacks it with her paw,

and the ball flies across the floor.

"Hooray!" Mitzy scurries after it. "Again!"

"She wouldn't fetch with me," Dustin says sadly.

"Call her," his mom suggests. "See if she comes."

"Here, Snowball!" Dustin chirps. "Come here, Snowball!" Mitzy keeps rubbing her nose over the grooves of her ball, ignoring him. Dustin's lips spread into a thin line. "Here, Mitzy!" he tries again. "Let's go, Mitzy!"

Mitzy raises her ears higher, but she doesn't get up.

"He's calling you," Gus prompts her. "He's using your real name. Go."

Mitzy flops onto her bed. "No."

Dustin's mom sighs. "Mitzy

wasn't acting the same with us. She didn't want to eat or explore or have fun."

"And she wouldn't sleep in bed with me," Dustin adds.

"She seemed nervous at our apartment," his mom continues. "She sat in a corner and whimpered to herself. But then when we came here this morning, she turned back into the perky dog Dustin fell in love with."

"Is that true?" Luna asks, and Mitzy drops her face with shame.

"You wanted to run and jump and fetch," Buttons reminds her. "You wanted someone to play with you."

"I still do," Mitzy says quietly. "But I missed it here."

"I may know the problem," Ted says. "Mitzy and Luna came from the same home. Their last owner

dropped them off at the shelter with one toy each: Mitzy with her ball and Luna with her mouse. The two of them have never been apart before. I didn't realize that Mitzy's missing Luna might be an issue."

"I see." Dustin's mom rests her hand on the boy's shoulder. "What do you think?"

"Can we take both for the rest of the weekend?" Dustin asks. "If Luna is Mitzy's best friend, then maybe we can become friends too."

His mom shakes her head. "Two pets are more than we can handle, even for a couple of days," she says gently. "Especially when one of them scratches and bites."

Dustin kneels on the ground near Mitzy. "I loved having Mitzy stay with us, but I want her to be happy. And she seems happier with Luna."

Ted nods. "I understand. You're welcome to come take her for walks whenever you like."

"Yes!" Mitzy scrambles over to Dustin. "Come every day to see me! We will still be friends!"

Dustin smiles. "I'd like that."

"And as you saw," Ted continues, "when you're ready to try again, we have plenty of other dogs available, both for fostering and for adoption."

"Do you want to take a look now?" Dustin's mom asks. "Just to see?"

"Okay," Dustin agrees. He pats

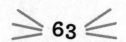

Mitzy's head before helping her into her cage. "I'll visit you later. I promise."

"That is an excellent promise!" Mitzy calls as Dustin follows his mom and Ted into the back room. Once they're gone, she spots something squished under her bed. "Oooh, maybe there is a treat!" Mitzy digs the object out from beneath the cushion. "Luna, it is your mouse! Here." She tosses the toy through the grate and then sticks her tongue toward Luna's

face. "Now come closer. Your ears are filthy."

"BLECH," Luna meows. But ever so slightly, she leans over until Mitzy's tongue skims the flap of her ear. And in her own way, Luna welcomes Mitzy home.

Word List

affectionate (uh•FEK•shuh•nuht): Showing love and fondness for someone

exhales (eks•HAILS): Breathes out

experiment (eks•PEHR•ih•ment): A test

feisty (FIHY•stee): Tough and aggressive

filthy (FILL•thee): Very dirty

genius (JEEN•yus): Very smart

intruder (in•TROO•dur): Someone

who goes where they are not invited

resembles (rih•ZEM•bulls): Looks like

responsibility (rih•SPAHN•suh•BIHL•ih•tee): A task or duty

silent (SIHY•lent): Without any noise

Questions

1. What part of Luna's body does Mitzy most like to clean?

2. What is Gus secretly afraid of?

3. Have you ever forgotten to pack a favorite toy? How did you feel without it?

4. What name does Dustin call Mitzy?

5. Why are Mitzy and Luna especially attached to each other?

6. Which pet from Whiskers Down the Lane would you most like to adopt? Why?